Meet DUKE & BRODY!

Melody A. Cooper

Tellwell Talent
www.tellwell.ca

ISBN
978-0-2288-3670-4 (Hardcover)
978-0-2288-1557-0 (Paperback)

This book is dedicated to my husband who makes it possible for me to follow my dreams.

This is Duke

and this is Brody.

Duke and Brody are very different,
but later realize they have more
in common than they think!

Duke is a big dog with big paws.
He is furry and golden white
with a deep rumbly bark.

Brody is a small dog with small paws. He has short brown hair and a very loud shrill bark.

Duke loves the cold weather.
While Brody enjoys the heat.

When they first met Duke wasn't very nice to Brody. He would bite and nip at him and chase him around the garden!

This frightened little Brody
because Duke is so much
larger than him and his
teeth are big and sharp.

But slowly as time passed
they grew closer...

They shared secrets
with each other...

They noticed they liked many of the same activities... Chasing squirrels, burying bones, chewing on sticks and digging up all sorts of treasures.

They began to sleep next to each other on the big fluffy bed. Often Duke would put his paw around Brody and would hold him as they slept. He protected Brody and made him feel safe.

In the morning they would eat their breakfast next to each other, and in the evening they would eat their dinner next to each other.

When it came time to play in the garden, Duke was more gentle and played in a way that made Brody feel more comfortable.

They were taken out for walks
together and enjoyed the
sights that surrounded them
in their neighborhood.

Now they run around the garden with big smiles on their faces, doing all of their favorite things together!

Duke and Brody are a team.

They are best friends.

They are brothers.

~ THE END ~

Lightning Source UK Ltd.
Milton Keynes UK
UKHW051348310720
367426UK00004B/135